Ringo
The Flamingo

Neil Griffiths

Illustrated by Judith Blake

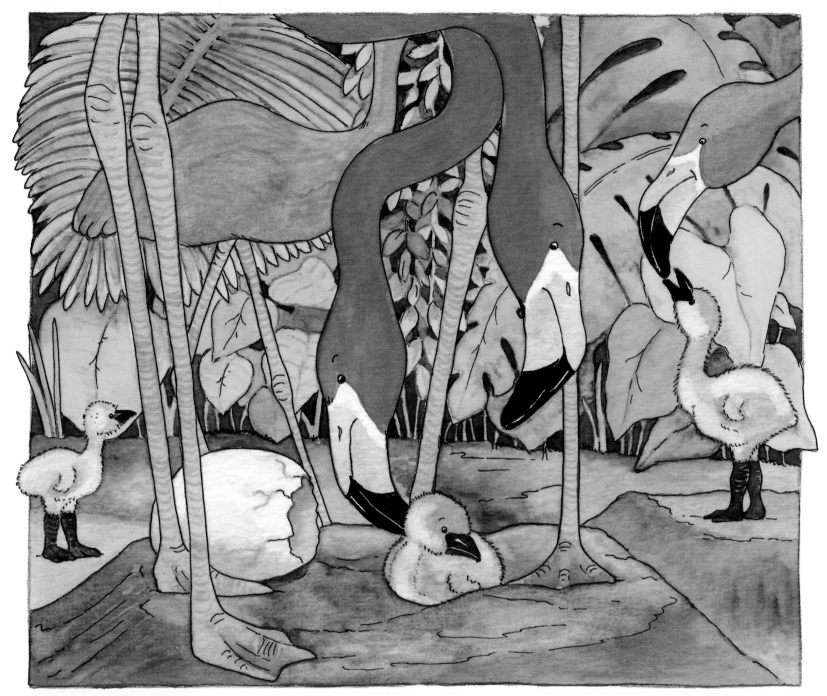

From the moment Ringo hatched from his large, white egg, his mother and father knew that something was wrong. The other flamingo chicks were already standing and plodding along behind their parents.

This book is dedicated to Gwen Metcalfe
and the special children at
Westlea Primary School, Swindon.

Red Robin Books is an imprint of Corner To Learn Limited

Published by
Corner To Learn Limited
Willow Cottage • 26 Purton Stoke
Swindon • Wiltshire SN5 4JF • UK

ISBN-13: 978-1-905434-06-0
ISBN-10: 1-905434-06-5

First published in the UK 2003
New edition published in the UK 2006
Text © Neil Griffiths 2003
Illustrations © Judith Blake 2003

Design by
David Rose

Printed by
Gutenberg Press Limited, Malta

Ringo did not stand up. No matter how hard he tried, he couldn't seem to make his legs move. His mother and father did all they could to help him up, but it was no use. Ringo would never be able to stand up or walk, as he had hatched with legs that simply didn't work.

In the days, months and years that followed, Ringo's parents took great care of him. They kept him fed well with freshwater shrimps, snuggled up close to him during the cooler nights and brought water in their large beaks for drinking and washing himself.

Ringo was usually very happy, and his cheerful nature helped him make friends and become a popular member of the flock. The other flamingoes would often visit him and tell wonderful stories of their long journeys across Africa and of the places they had seen.

They also helped him to move by huddling
together and lifting him into the shade, or to
a new spot of his choice along the lakeside.

Ringo loved their company, but there were also times when he liked to be alone, as they did tend to fuss and spoil him. Sometimes all he wanted to do was sit quietly and think. The other flamingoes understood and knew when he needed a little time to himself.

It was during moments like this that Ringo occasionally felt very sad. He would watch the other flamingoes and wish he could march like tall soldiers as they did, or race across the surface of the lake and sweep high into the bright blue sky.

But he couldn't.

Life around the lake was always very busy with flamingoes constantly flying in and out. Ringo loved to watch the comings and goings, and knew every flamingo in the flock.

However, on one particular day, a stranger arrived who Ringo had never seen before. He had flown in from across the plains. He took one look at Ringo and began to laugh at his little legs and make fun of his tiny feet. This made Ringo very sad and angry inside, but he tried not to show it.

As soon as the flock heard
what was going on, they
marched the stranger off
and he was never seen again.

Days around the lakeside changed very little, but there was one that Ringo and the flock would never forget.

It all began as it usually did. Ringo was sitting on the shore, sipping beakfuls of cool water. The other flamingoes were busy, as they always were at this time of day, sifting for shrimps in the shallows.

Ringo was the first to notice that something was different.
The sky was redder than he had ever seen it before at sunrise.
The rays of sunlight seemed to be dancing wildly in the sky.

"Fire! Fire!"
shrieked a passing flamingo.
"Fire! Fire!"

The whole flock panicked and took flight into the sky, leaving Ringo stranded and alone.

The flames grew closer and closer and Ringo became more and more frightened. The air was thick with smoke, and scorching hot.

But Ringo was not alone. Through the smoke he could see a tiny chick quivering on a nest nearby; its mother must have left it as the flock began to panic. He knew he must protect it from the heat and flames, but how could he get to it?

Using all his strength, he stretched out his neck and pulled his body across the shoreline by digging his beak into the sticky mud and flapping his wings. Finally, although exhausted, he reached the little chick and tucked it under his tummy feathers.

By now, the flames were so close that
they began to scorch Ringo's tail feathers
and burn his skin, but he didn't move. He
kept the chick safe beneath his wing.

Then just as it looked as if Ringo would be smothered
by the flames, they began to die down. The wet mud
along the lakeside had dampened the fire, and soon
it was completely out.

Knowing it was now safe, the flock returned to find Ringo, a little scorched and covered in soot, but with a great big smile on his face!
"How could he be smiling at a time like this?" they thought.

"Look!" said Ringo, as out from beneath his wing popped the fluffy chick. The whole flock cheered and told Ringo how brave he was. He felt so proud.

The chick's mother had been so frightened that she did not return to the lakeside, so Ringo adopted the chick as his very own. It loved Ringo very much and he took great care of it.

Ringo's bravery was never forgotten. The flock would often leave their chicks with him for safety while they went in search of food, or tuck an egg under his tummy to keep warm for them. In fact, Ringo became chief egg and chick sitter!

This made Ringo feel very special, and nothing made him happier than the wriggling and chirping of tiny chicks beneath his warm feathers.

The end

Other books by Neil Griffiths:

Who'd be a fly?
The story of a very hungry fly catcher
by Neil Griffiths
Illustrated by Doug Nash

Messy Martin
by Neil Griffiths
Illustrated by Doug Nash

Itchy Bear
Neil Griffiths

The Journey
by Neil Griffiths and Scott Mann
Illustrated by Judith Blake

The Scarecrow Who Didn't Scare
by Neil Griffiths
Illustrated by Vicki Leigh

Winnie Wagtail
Neil Griffiths
Illustrated by Eileen Browne

No room for a baby roo!
by Neil Griffiths
Illustrated by Doug Nash

Walter's Windy Washing Line
by Neil Griffiths
Illustrated by Judith Blake

Florence was no ordinary Fairy
Neil Griffiths
Illustrated by Doug Nash

If Only...
Neil Griffiths
Illustrated by Judith Blake

Mrs Rainbow
by Neil Griffiths
Illustrated by Judith Blake

Grandma Brown's Three Fine Pigs
by Neil Griffiths
Illustrated by Judith Blake

Did you see them too?
Neil Griffiths

Red Robin BOOKS
Where story matters
www.redrobinbooks.com